CARGO TRUCK

RUNWAY CLEANER

BELT LOADER

T0376119

For Mom and Dad
– T. K.

For Papá and Juan
– N. R. C.

First edition published in 2025 by Flying Eye Books,
27 Westgate Street, London, E8 3RL.
www.flyingeyebooks.com

Represented by: Authorised Rep Compliance Ltd.
Ground Floor, 71 Lower Baggot Street, Dublin, D02 P593, Ireland.
www.arccompliance.com

Text © Tori Kosara 2025
Illustrations © Natalia Rojas Castro 2025

1 3 5 7 9 10 8 6 4 2

Edited by Fay Evans
Designed by Lilly Gottwald

ISBN: 978-1-83874-922-4

Published in the US by Flying Eye Books Ltd.
Printed in Poland on FSC® certified paper.

MIX
Paper | Supporting
responsible forestry
FSC® C163799
FSC
www.fsc.org

THE GOOD NIGHT AIRPORT

Tori Kosara • Natalia Rojas Castro

Flying Eye Books

Clock chimes are ringing through the town.
The tired sun is going down.

These workers wave off one last flight.
It's time for them to say good night.

When Motor Isle goes to bed,
The Good Night Airport wakes instead.
These great machines will work all night,
To keep this airport running right.

Inside the hangar, machines stir,
Their noisy engines start to whir.
While the full moon begins to glow,
The vehicles prepare to go.

Beacons turn on with a flash.
Come on team! We have to dash!

Aircraft land on this strip all day,
But now the planes have come to stay.

Their tires leave bits of rubber here.
Runway Cleaner gets asphalt clear.

Powerful nozzles spray the ground,
While scrubbing heads whiz round and round.
Debris shoots up the vacuum hose—
Into the holding tank it goes!

Woosh
Woosh

Runway Cleaner gives tarmac grip.
Now landing airplanes will not slip.

Here's helpful Lavatory Truck,
To clean out this plane's toilet muck.
The waste tank filled up on the flight.
It's time to get it clean and bright!

Raise the platform to the full tank.
Open the hatch with a pull—*YANK!*

Hook up the hose. The waste drains out,
Into the truck's tank through a spout.

Plane toilets will not overflow,
Because this truck's a cleaning pro.

Belt Loader rolls onto the tarmac,
To help the cargo craft unpack.
The planes haul goods to Motor Isle.
Belt Loader unloads freight in style.

Drive up to the open bay door,
And tilt the boom a little more.
The belt carries loads from the bay.
Then cargo trucks drive it away.

Important goods are sent to town.
Belt Loader won't let the Isle down!

Air ambulance waits patiently,
To aid in an emergency.
If there's a call for help tonight,
This helicopter will take flight.

THWUP
THWUP
THWUP

Time for takeoff! Let's go, night crew.
Turn on the lights and engine, too.
The rotors spin. They're in the air!
This craft flies to deliver care.

Motor Isle need never worry—
Copters rescue in a hurry.

When a plane's in need of repair,
Tow Tractor helps the craft get there.
At the hangar, engineers wait,
While this tug hauls its hefty freight.

CHUG, CHUG

Lower down the vehicle ramp.
Cradle the plane's wheel with a clamp.
Slowly pull the aircraft along.
Now mechanics can fix what's wrong.

Tractor moves planes with all its might,
So aircraft can be mended at night.

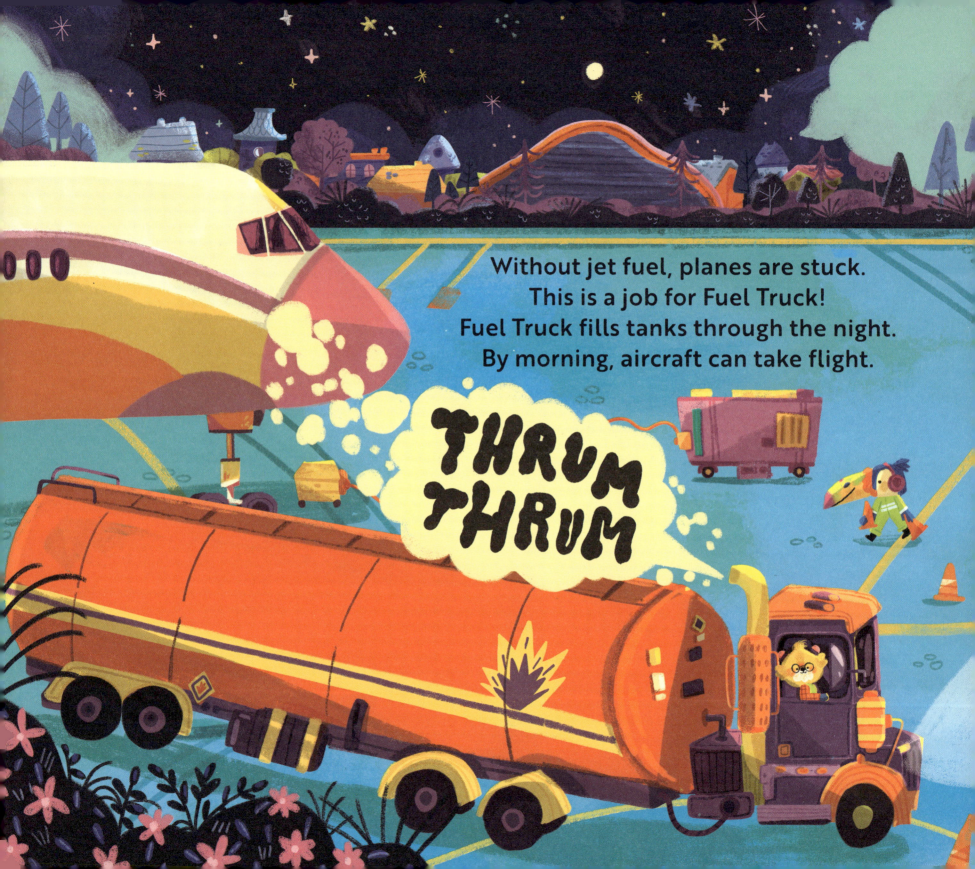

Without jet fuel, planes are stuck.
This is a job for Fuel Truck!
Fuel Truck fills tanks through the night.
By morning, aircraft can take flight.

THRUM THRUM

Secure the fuel nozzle—*CLICK.*
Switch on the gas pump with a flick.
Fuel gushes into the plane.
Soon the gauge will say "full" again.

If tanks are empty, planes can't fly.
Thanks to this truck, they'll reach the sky!

The stars grow dim. So does the moon.
The airport will be open soon.
But planes can't leave without fresh meals.
Catering Truck brings food on wheels.

Beep Beep!

Strong stabilizers hit the floor.
The body raises to the door.
Press a button. Out the ramp slides.
Onto the plane, the food cart glides.

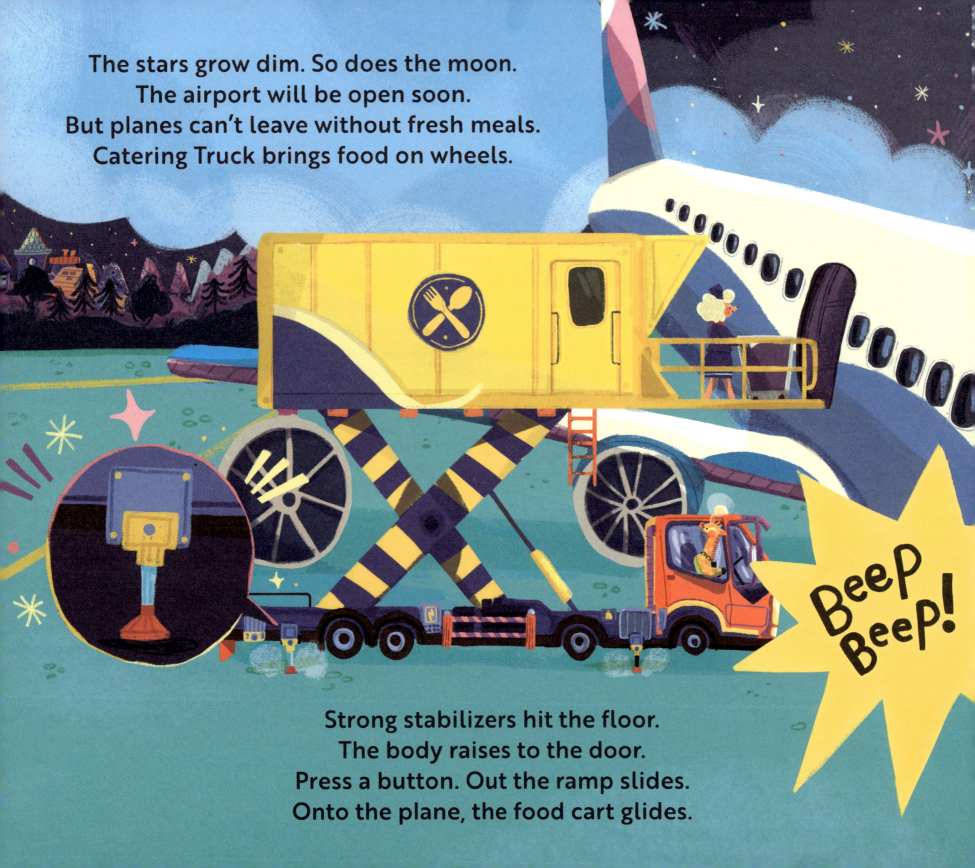

Catering Truck brings jets supplies;
Feeding passengers in the skies.

Plane engines start. The sky grows bright.
The daytime team is now in sight.
Good Night Airport, your jobs are done.
Roll off to bed beneath the sun.

You've worked so hard the whole night through.
And you deserve a good rest, too.
Close up the hangar. Say sweet dreams.
You'll wake to the shine of soft moonbeams.

DEPARTURES

Snuggle up, machines. Sleep tight.
Good Night Airport, see you tonight.

LAVATORY TRUCK

AIR AMBULANCE

CATERING TRUCK

TOW TRACTOR

FUEL TRUCK